Tyler Jordan

INLINE SKATER

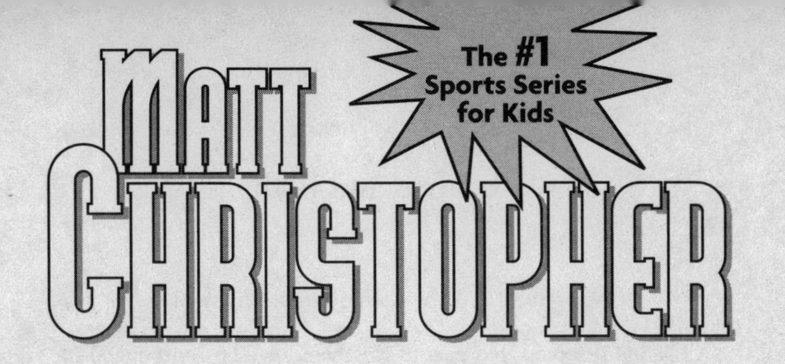

INLINE SKATER

Text by Robert Hirschfeld

Little, Brown and Company
Boston New York London

To Chris and Beth

First Paperback Edition

Matt Christopher™ is a trademark of Catherine M. Christopher.

Text by Robert Hirschfeld

Library of Congress Cataloging-in-Publication Data

Hirschfeld, Robert.
Inline skater / text by Robert Hirschfeld. — 1st ed.
p. cm.
"Matt Christopher."
Summary: Cris must choose between "aggro" skating and roller hockey, which also means choosing between his old friends and some new ones.
ISBN 0-316-12071-5 (hc) — ISBN 0-316-12144-4 (pb)
[1. In-line skating — Fiction. 2. Roller hockey — Fiction. 3. Friendship — Fiction.] I. Title.
PZ7.H59794 In 2001
[Fic] — dc21 00-059821

10 9 8 7 6 5 4 3 2

COM-MO

Printed in the United States of America

What could be better, thought Cris Murphy as he bent down to fasten a buckle on his in-line skate, *than running some cool moves in a halfpipe on a sunny Saturday afternoon?*

Nothing, that's what. His best friend, Max Pellington, shot off the top of the halfpipe like a bullet, spun around in a dazzling 540, a full one and a half rotations, and swooped back down the side, perfectly balanced.

The halfpipe looked like a giant, fifteen-foot length of concrete water main that had been sliced in half lengthwise. It was part of a recreation area set aside for skaters and skateboarders. In addition to halfpipes, it featured some ramps and rails — like the handrails found on stairs — on which kids could show off their best maneuvers.

Cris and Max, both twelve years old, were big fans of this kind of stunt skating, known as "aggressive" skating, or "aggro" for short. Along with a few friends, they had made this park their weekend hangout and spent a lot of after-school time here as well.

"Come on, dude," Max yelled, turning to Cris. "Let's see your Royale!"

Cris was tall for his age, with exceptional coordination. He grinned and skated toward a rail sitting on three-foot-high posts. He raced forward, pumping to build up speed. Just before the rail, he leaped high.

"Yeah!" Max yelled. "Catch some air!"

Cris planted the inside edge of his right, or leading, skate on the rail, hitting the rail exactly on the "grind plate" — a grooved plate between the middle wheels — and cocking his left leg so the trailing edge of the left skate slid along the rail. Using his arms for balance, he slid the length of the rail, leaping off at the end. He came down lightly, swung around, and headed back to his friends.

"Awesome!" Doog, a skinny boy with a broad grin, held out a hand for Cris to slap.

"Hey, your Royale is getting pretty near as good as mine," said Max, without cracking a smile. Max was powerfully built and wore his light brown hair in a buzz cut.

"Dream on," Cris replied. "You'll never catch the air *I* do. You're not bad, for a chunkster, but —"

Max let out a yell and grabbed his friend's head in a playful wrestling hold. "*Chunkster?* You *dweeb* . . ."

Doog poked Max. "Yo, check it out."

A new kid had skated up, wearing neither helmet nor pads. As he approached, Cris called, "Hey, where's your armor?"

The new guy turned. "Armor?" he repeated, with a sneer on his face.

Cris gestured to the helmet and heavy pads that protected his knees, elbows, and wrists. His friends wore the same gear.

The new guy shook his head. "Don't need it. That stuff is for wimps."

Max snickered. "This dude is going to learn about pain if he isn't very careful . . . and very good."

Cris shook his head. "We shouldn't let him mess around here without pads. If someone gets hurt bad, people say, 'See? That aggro stuff is dangerous.' Let's tell him —"

"Too late," Doog pointed out. "Cross your fingers."

The new guy poised at the edge of the

halfpipe and headed down, backward—“fakie” in the language of aggro skating—facing back the way he had come.

“Fakie 360, I bet,” Max said, meaning that the guy would speed up the other side of the halfpipe, launch himself high, and try to spin in a full circle before coming back down.

“Maybe he *is* really good,” Cris said.

“I don’t think so,” Max replied as the kid in the halfpipe began to flail his arms awkwardly. “Watch *out!*”

The guy managed to break his fall with one outstretched hand, but still came down hard on his unprotected knees and rolled to the bottom of the concrete surface.

Cris winced in sympathy and raced toward the fallen skater. “You all right?” he asked as the stranger struggled to stand.

“Take it easy,” cautioned Doog, but the boy waved off their help and got to his feet.

The right knee of his jeans was ripped and Cris could see a bloody scrape through the tear. The palms of his hands were also a mess — but he was able to stand and didn't appear to have been seriously hurt.

"Better get that cleaned up," Max advised. The boy limped away silently.

"That was truly *dumb,*" Doog said as they watched him leave. "He's lucky he didn't break anything."

Cris nodded. "Yeah. You have to be crazy to do aggro moves without armor."

"Speaking of wimps . . . ," said Max, jerking his thumb at a group of kids skating past. Their skates were different, with larger wheels and no grind plates, and they carried hockey sticks. There was a rink for roller hockey at the other end of the park, and this group was headed that way.

"Yo, better be careful with those sticks," Max called out. "You might hurt each other!"

"Yeah," Doog shouted, "don't trip over a puck!" He snickered. "What a lame game!"

"For sure," echoed Max.

Feeling uncomfortable, Cris said nothing. His dad had played professional ice hockey — in the minor leagues — and his seventeen-year-old brother, Greg, played both ice and roller hockey, too. They'd been urging Cris to give the game a try.

Of course, there was no *way* he'd say anything about it to Max, knowing how his friend would react to the notion.

"Whoa, it's getting late," Max said, checking the wristwatch he'd left on the ground with his schoolbooks. "I better go. You coming, Cris?"

"Uh, I have someplace to go first. See you tomorrow, okay?"

"See you," Max said. Doog waved to Cris as he skated away with Max. Cris waited until they disappeared around a corner. Then he headed toward the area of the park that was marked off as a hockey rink.

There he saw a group of kids about his age having a practice session. They were in two lines, moving up and down the rink and circling around some orange traffic cones. Off to one side stood a man in a sweatshirt with a whistle around his neck.

The man clapped. "*Leo!* Flex the knees! *That's* right! Tight turns, everyone!"

After a minute, he whistled and the players began a drill involving passing pucks back and forth. They seemed to be working hard, but they were also enjoying themselves. Cris saw that they were skillful skaters, though maybe not as fast as he and his friends.

Watching a drill in which they skated backward and did more tight turns and pivots, Cris decided that they were much better at some skating skills than he was.

A few minutes later, the guy in the sweatshirt, evidently their coach, whistled and told them to take a break. One of them skated over to Cris. Cris worried that the boy might think he had been one of the guys who jeered earlier, but he seemed friendly enough.

"Those are cool skates," he said, pointing to Cris's feet. "You into aggro?"

"Yeah," Cris said. "It's really neat. You ever try it? You're a good enough skater, it looks like. I'm Cris Murphy."

The other boy smiled. "Barry Dillon. I don't know . . . it looks tough. I'd *like* to do some of those moves, but they're a little scary."

Cris laughed. "Scary?"

"Yeah!" Barry stared at Cris. "You've never been scared to try some of that stuff? When you spin upside down, and you're, like, ten feet in the air . . . with no *net*?"

Cris admired the fact that Barry wasn't ashamed to admit to being scared. He wondered if he could say the same thing to Max, and how Max would react.

"Well," Cris said, "yeah, I guess I used to get scared, especially when I was first learning the moves. But now, I don't think about it. I don't know if I could do some of what *you* do — those fast turns. I'd get dizzy."

Now Barry laughed. "It's funny, I never think about *that.*"

The coach's whistle cut off the chat. "Well, I better get back," said Barry. "Nice meeting you, Cris. See you around, I hope."

"Me, too," Cris answered, and started for home. He thought about hockey, and whether he should take a shot at it. It might be fun, and Barry was a nice guy. Whatever Max thought, no way was Barry a wuss.

He frowned, imagining the grief Max and Doog and the aggro bunch would give him when — if — he told them he was going to play roller hockey.

It would be a bad scene. And those dudes were his friends. It was a definite problem, for which, right at the moment, he had no clear answer.

When Cris sat down for breakfast the next morning, his parents and his brother all wore big grins, as if they were ready to spring a big, happy surprise on him.

"What's up?" he asked as he poured some juice. "Why all the big smiles? I know it's not my birthday, or anything like that."

"I have some news I think you're going to like," said Mr. Murphy, smiling even wider. "Remember my old buddy Harp Sanders? From my playing days?"

"Harp?" repeated Cris. "Oh, yeah, wasn't

he the goalie on your old team? The guy who you said was so tough?"

Mr. Murphy nodded. "Toughest man I ever met. He'd stand up to anyone in that crease. Harp would have played goal *without* a mask if he had to."

"I don't know if that's being tough or being foolish," Mrs. Murphy said.

With a sigh, Mr. Murphy went on. "The point is, Harp was a great teammate. Anyway, I found out he's coaching a roller hockey team here . . . kids your age, Cris. Team's called the Hawks. So I called him up last night."

Cris felt a sinking feeling, knowing what was coming and not knowing how he'd respond. "Oh, yeah? What about?"

"About you playing hockey, like your old man used to. Anyway, Harp would like to meet you and have you try out for the team."

"Isn't that great?" Greg asked. "You're going to love hockey, I guarantee it. And I bet you'll be really good at it, too."

Mrs. Murphy, who never made a secret of her dislike of aggro skating, put her hand on Cris's shoulder. "I know how you love to skate, and I never complain about that" — she made a face as if she'd just bit into a very sour lemon — "*aggressive* thing you do. But I keep expecting you to break an arm or a leg."

"*Mom* . . . ," Cris said, carefully keeping his voice calm. "I told you, I always wear pads and a helmet. I'm not going to hurt myself."

"I'd still feel better knowing you're playing hockey," insisted Mrs. Murphy. "Maybe I'm just being silly, but . . ."

"The thing is," Greg interrupted, "why not give it a shot? It's not like we're sentencing you to jail. Hockey is great! Till you try it, how do you know if you like it or not?"

Mr. Murphy leaned forward. "What do you say, Slugger? What do I tell Harp?"

Cris felt trapped. *What do* I *tell Max?* he thought to himself. But when his father used that nickname, "Slugger," a name he'd been using since Cris was a baby, Cris knew that there could be only one answer.

"Tell him I'll try out. But if I don't like it, I may not keep doing it, all right?"

Mr. Murphy spread his arms wide. "Sure! But you're going to love it. I'll call Harp tonight."

"Great," Cris said, trying to look happy.

It wasn't a school day, so after breakfast, Greg found Cris in the yard, sitting in a lawn chair, staring at nothing in particular.

"Hey, bro, can I join you?"

Cris waved to another chair, and Greg sat

down. "How come you're so down on hockey, anyway?" he asked. "I mean, I know you're into aggro skating big time, but that doesn't mean you have to hate hockey, too."

"I *don't* hate hockey!" Cris shouted. "Did I ever say I hated hockey? Did I?"

"Whoa!" Greg blinked in surprise. "No, you're right. Then why don't you want to try out for this team? I don't get it."

Cris shook his head. "It's going to sound really dumb."

"Try me," urged his brother.

Cris hesitated for a second and then took the plunge. "It's my friends, all right? Max and those guys. I mean, Max is my best friend, and he thinks hockey is strictly for wimps. What'll he say when I tell him I'm playing hockey? Max will give me grief forever."

"I see the problem," Greg said. "It's no fun being dissed by your pals, I know. Are you sure that's what they'd say?"

Cris nodded. "Absolutely. No question."

Greg didn't say anything for a moment. Then he reached out and tapped his brother on the arm. "I want you to think about a couple of things, okay? First of all, I really believe that, once you start playing hockey, you're going to really get into it. If you don't . . . well, like Dad says, forget it. Dad'll understand.

"Also, playing a team sport is different. You'll get to know new people, probably make new friends. Not just friends, *teammates.* There's something about being part of a team, it's hard to explain, but . . . when you're part of a team, you know the other guys will be there for you, they'll back you up, and you'll be there for them. There's nothing like it. You have to experience it to see what I'm talking about."

Greg stood up. "One other thing. If Max really *is* a good friend, he won't stop being a friend just because you try a new sport. If he *does* stop being your friend, I'd say that he wasn't as good a friend as you thought."

Cris nodded. "Okay. You're right."

Greg grinned. "Good man."

That afternoon, Cris was at the park with Max, watching Doog skimming along a rail on one skate, his outstretched hand gripping the skate on his other foot — a so-called "Fishbrain."

"All right *Doog!*" yelled Max. He poked Cris's arm. "Smooth move!"

"Totally," Cris agreed. He kneeled down to adjust a buckle, and said, in a casual voice, "Hey, I was thinking . . ."

"Uh-oh," said Max. "That's dangerous when you haven't done it much."

"Ha ha," Cris muttered. "No, really, I was talking with Greg the other day, and he was talking about hockey. He's been playing for a long time, and he's going to play in college, and . . . well, I don't know, maybe it isn't such a wimpy thing to do."

Max turned and stared at Cris in disbelief. "You're kidding, right?"

Cris shrugged. "I only thought —"

Max rolled his eyes. "Look at the uniforms they wear! Majorly ugly! And shoving that dumb puck around with those stupid sticks . . . no *way!* Face facts, my man. Hockey is for geeks who are afraid to do their own thing, who have to do it with a bunch of other geeks. But for cool dudes like us? Forget it!"

Cris gave up. Max wasn't going to change his mind, it was clear.

"How come you're asking?" asked Max, giving Cris a curious look.

"No reason," replied Cris quickly.

"Good," said Max. "It's too nice a day to be talking about hockey."

"Yeah, I guess," said Cris, unhappily.

Here we are," said Cris, looking around nervously at the rink. "We must be early."

It was the day on which he was to meet Harp and the Hawk's hockey team, and Cris was not looking forward to it. When Greg had offered to come along for moral support, Cris had been happy to accept.

There were a bunch of kids on the rink, doing some kind of warmup drill, zigging back and forth, passing pucks around, and chatting among themselves. Watching them, Cris thought he'd have no trouble learning the game; he was a good athlete, and what aggro skaters call a "blur" — a very fast skater, way faster than what he was seeing on the rink.

Barry Dillon caught sight of Cris and gave him a friendly wave, but kept skating with the others.

Cris hoped that his aggro friends wouldn't spot him there. Some of them might very well pass by on their way to their part of the park.

Cris looked down at the skates his brother had given him. They looked pretty bad, he thought, with wheels that were huge compared to the ones on his regular skates. They were "rockered," meaning that the front and back wheels on each skate didn't touch the ground when the middle wheels did. It had felt weird at first, but Greg said that rockering made hockey skates more maneuverable in turns.

Greg had also loaned him a hockey stick, an old wooden one. He said that if Cris stayed with the sport, he'd probably want to get his own stick and might prefer one made of aluminum or graphite.

The man Cris had seen working with the team when he'd watched their practice now showed up and whistled for attention. A minute later the kids began doing a more organized drill, in which they skated in single file, in zigzag lines, up and down the rink. Cris glanced at Greg. "Bo-o-o-ring," he whispered.

Greg looked a little annoyed. "Hey, it's just a warmup," he said.

A few minutes later the group began a new drill, in which they skated fast in a straight line, stopped abruptly and pivoted to the left, then skated forward, stopped and pivoted to the right, and so forth. Compared with catching air in the halfpipe, this was kiddie stuff. Cris was beginning to wish he'd never agreed to come, when the man came over to him and his brother.

"You must be Cris Murphy. I'm Harp Sanders." He looked at Greg, who introduced himself. "Oh, yeah, I saw you play a couple of high school games last season. You remind me of your dad — and that's a compliment."

He cupped his hands and called, "Steve! See you a minute?"

A rugged dark-haired boy skated over. Harp gestured to Cris. "Steve, meet Cris Murphy, who's going to try out for the Hawks. Cris, this is Steve Cimino, the Hawks' captain."

"Hi," Cris said.

"Hi," replied Steve. "You ever play any hockey?"

Cris shook his head. "I'm into aggro."

"Uh-huh." Steve didn't seem impressed.

Well, thought Cris, *I'm not impressed with these dudes, either.*

Steve looked Cris up and down. "He's too skinny for a defenseman. Maybe he could be a forward — if he has speed and coordination."

Without a word, Cris raced out on the rink and sped down one side, pumping his arms to build up speed. *If I have speed, huh?* he thought. *Check this out, pal.* He swung around, noting that turns *were* easier with rockered wheels, and raced back to the others. As he stopped, he saw that Steve still wasn't impressed and that his brother looked a little embarrassed.

"Uh-huh," Steve said, his voice flat. "Now, try it again — with *this* in your hand," he said, holding out Greg's old hockey stick.

Cris was startled; he'd forgotten about the stick. He took it and started again. But the edge of the stick scraped the ground and he stumbled. When he held it off the ground in both hands, he couldn't pump his arms to build up speed. When he held it in one hand, it got very heavy very fast. He came back feeling foolish and noticed that a few Hawks were grinning at him. One actually snickered. Barry just looked at him, neither smiling nor laughing.

"Wait till you've got a puck to handle," said Steve. "It may not be aggro skating, but it's not as easy as you think, either."

"Guess not," Cris admitted, wishing he could crawl into a hole and vanish for a month or so.

"But he'll pick it up, you'll see," said Greg, stepping forward. "I'm his brother, and I know how athletic Cris is. It won't take long."

"I'm sure Cris is a good athlete," said

Harp, "and he might make a good hockey player — if he wants to make a real commitment to learning the game." He faced Cris. "You'll have a lot to pick up: stick handling, passing, defense, understanding what it is to be on a team. Think you want to do that?"

"Think you *can* do that?" asked Steve.

Cris felt a sudden urge to show Steve, to show all of them, that anything they could do, he could do, too. At first, it hadn't seemed like much, but now he saw that it would be a challenge. The Hawks had all been playing hockey for a while, and he was new to it. It would take time.

Did he really want to?

Before he could answer, he saw Max and Doog skate past, along with a couple of their friends. He froze. Had they seen him? What would they say if they had seen him?

Harp saw Cris hesitate and said, "Maybe you need a day to think it over. We'll be here tomorrow afternoon, same time, same place. If you show up, ready to work, then we'll give you a chance to prove yourself. If not . . . we'll assume you decided to pass. Okay?"

"Sure," said Cris. Harp nodded, patted Cris on the shoulder, and walked away.

Steve turned to go, stopped, and turned back to Cris. "By the way, I did a little aggro skating, too. Probably you're better at it than me, but I did it. Then I gave it up and switched to hockey, and I think I made the right choice . . . right for *me,* anyway. I don't know if it's right for you. Guess your aggro buddies don't think much of it, the way they were giving us grief the other day."

Surprised, Cris stared at the other boy.

"Right. I was one of the guys your friends were laughing at — like some of *these* guys were laughing at you just now. But you didn't join in, which makes me think you're not a creep. Come back tomorrow and check it out. What have you got to lose?"

Cris shrugged. "Nothing . . . I guess."

He and Greg started home. *I don't* think *I have anything to lose,* Cris thought. *Unless I lose some friends.*

So . . . have you decided?" Greg was driving to school the day after Cris had (in his opinion) made a fool of himself in front of the Hawks. Cris had expected Greg's question, and still had no idea what he was going to do.

Stopped at a red light, Greg looked at Cris, who avoided his eyes.

"What's the big deal?" Greg asked, pulling away from the light. "Seems to me you're making a mountain out of a molehill."

"Okay, okay," Cris snapped. "I'm going. You happy now?"

Greg slapped the steering wheel. "Hey,

the idea isn't to make *me* happy, or Dad happy. It's to make *you* happy. And if that means not doing something because you're afraid of what your friends will say . . . then skip it."

"I'm not afraid!" yelled Cris. Greg didn't say a word, and after a moment Cris said, more quietly, "Sorry. But I'm not afraid."

"No?" Greg asked, his eyes on the road. "Okay, you're not afraid. You're making this a major hassle for some other reason. Cool."

Cris slumped down in the seat. "No, you're right. I am . . . I'll go. I *will*."

Greg shook his head. "You'd think we were forcing you to spend a day at the dentist instead of playing a game."

Cris grinned. "I'm being totally dumb, aren't I? You're right, I'm going."

"Only if you want to," Greg said.

"Shut up," Cris said and laughed.

At lunch hour, Cris spotted Max and a couple of friends outside and headed their way. Max looked up and said, "Well, look who's here! It's Mr. Hockey!"

The other two laughed. Obviously, Max *had* seen Cris the day before. "What are you doing here with us aggro types?" Max asked, scowling. "Why don't you go sit with your hockey buddies? They're more your speed, right?"

Cris felt his face reddening. "What's that mean? I came to have lunch with *you.* You have a problem with that?"

"A problem?" echoed Max, with a glance at his friends, who were enjoying themselves watching. "*Nooo,* why should I have a problem? No, it's an honor to have a *hockey player* having lunch with us, right, guys?"

The others nodded and laughed, and Cris felt left out and alone . . . and angry. He spent hundreds of hours with these guys. They were supposed to be his friends. Why were they doing this?

Max went on, playing to his audience. "See, *hockey players* are too good to sit with us, so if Cris sits down, we should stand! Because *hockey players* wear *uniforms* and use *sticks* and say 'Please' and 'Excuse me' if they run into each other . . . which they do a lot."

Cris told himself to stay cool and not start yelling, or worse. That would be exactly what Max wanted. But it wasn't easy.

Finally, Max stopped and sneered at Cris. "Go find your hockey friends. We don't want you here."

"Okay," Cris said, really mad. "I *will.* I'm going to start playing with that hockey team this afternoon . . . and I *will* find new friends. Friends who don't pick on you just for trying something different. See you around . . . maybe."

Just before he walked away, Cris thought he saw Max look a little unsure of himself and start to say something, but he didn't stop to find out. He was too mad and didn't care *what* Max had to say or what he thought.

He would play hockey. And if Max didn't like it, well, that was just too bad.

He arrived later that day with Greg's old stick and skates and his own helmet. Harp looked at the equipment and said that it would do for the moment, but eventually, Cris would probably want to get his own gear, assuming he stuck it out with hockey. The coach called the team together and introduced Cris. Barry, with whom Cris had talked, smiled at him, and the guy who had openly laughed the day before gave Cris a hard stare, which Cris returned. Harp called Steve over and told him to work with Cris on basics while he, Harp, ran drills.

Steve began by having the Hawks introduce themselves. The guy who had laughed was Leo Austin, a powerful-looking redhead with bright blue eyes. Two of the Hawks, it turned out, were girls.

Before practice began, Leo came over. "I hear you're an aggro skater."

Cris nodded. Leo glared. "I don't like aggro skating . . . or the guys who do it."

Before Cris could decide how to respond, Steve stepped between them and stared at Leo. "It's time for practice," he said, and Leo, after giving Cris a final glare, turned away.

"What's *his* problem?" Cris demanded.

"Don't worry about him," advised Steve. "He can come on a little strong, but he's all right. You won't have any trouble with him . . . and he plays tough defense."

"I'll bet," Cris said, wondering whether Steve was right, or whether he and Leo might eventually have a bigger confrontation. But he decided to take Steve's advice and not worry about it.

Under Steve's guidance, Cris quickly picked up basic moves. There was the "swizzle," in which a player moved forward or backward by making **s** shapes with the inside edges of one or both skates. The one-foot swizzle was for circling, quick pivots, and quick stops. Cris learned how to cross one leg over the other going forward or backward and tried to learn how to make sudden changes of direction and shifts from skating forward to backward — important, Steve pointed out, on defense. And most basic of all, he practiced skating with a stick in hand, with and without a puck.

After almost an hour, Steve seemed satisfied with Cris's progress. Cris agreed to take a puck with him in order to practice at home. They joined the rest of the team for some drills.

The first drill in which Cris took part was a relay race, with players racing up and down the length of the rink as fast as possible while pushing a puck with the stick. Being new to it, Cris lost control a couple of times and cost his side the race.

"Yo, aggro-man," called Leo. "Why don't you go slide down a rail somewhere and leave hockey to people who can play?"

"Chill out, Leo," said Steve. "He's just learning, all right?"

"Yeah, really, Leo, you're just a cheap-shot artist!" snapped another player, a girl whose name Cris couldn't recall. "You're not so great, you know. You used to need an instruction sheet to tie your laces!" A few Hawks laughed. Leo gave the girl a sullen look, but didn't say anything else.

The girl came over to Cris, who was feeling bad about his showing in the race. "Take it easy," she said. "Don't give up. You'll pick it up soon."

Cris smiled gratefully. "Thanks, I appreciate it. What's your name, again?"

She took off her helmet, revealing glossy black hair cut short and straight. "Molly Hartnett. And Leo's all bark and no bite."

"I'll remember that," he said.

"This is a good group," said Molly, "and we're really into being a team. Even Leo, once you get to know him. And he never *really* needed instructions to tie his shoes . . . just a hint now and then."

Cris chuckled and decided he liked Molly. As practice went on, he relaxed and discovered that he was feeling more confident. He was even finding the stick easier to manage.

After some more drills, Harp blew his whistle. "All right, take five and we'll run a few three-on-three quickies. Cris, over here."

Cris skated over. "You need to spend time working on stick and puck handling," Harp said, "but you're doing all right. However, you're not ready for three-on-three. Stay here and watch, and I'll give you pointers, all right?"

Cris nodded, relieved that he hadn't made a mess of things. Harp chose two teams of three players; one put red jerseys on. The goals were unguarded, and Harp began play with a "face-off" — dropping the puck between a player from each team in the circle in the middle of the rink, then stepping back to watch.

"Watch Leo and Barry on defense," Harp said to Cris. "See how they try to force Steve and Molly outside, keep them away from their goal? The way they keep their heads on a swivel, always seeing that they know where the puck is, where their opponents are?

"Look! Molly faked toward the side and

cut inside Barry! Steve's pass set her up for a shot!" He whistled play to a halt.

"Barry!" he called. "You reacted too fast when Molly moved to her right! Stay to your opponent's inside on defense!"

Barry nodded. "I jumped the gun."

"Okay, let's set up again," Harp said, moving in for a face-off. This time, Leo, at center, got the puck, flipped a quick pass to Barry, and charged toward his opponents' goal. But Steve poked the puck away from Barry with a lunge of his stick and his team was quickly in position to score. Even Cris saw that Leo's charge had left him out of position to defend when the puck changed hands.

"Sorry," Leo called, looking embarrassed. "I shouldn't have done that."

"We've been through this," Harp said. "You have to fight the impulse to be an instant hero, or you'll wind up an instant goat. Okay?"

After a few minutes, Harp brought in fresh players, and the session went on. Cris realized that he was beginning to see the strategies: the importance of quick, accurate passes; the necessity of communication between players; the need to keep aware of where the puck is at all times, on offense or defense.

Molly, helmet under her arm, came over. "What do you think? You getting the idea?"

"Yeah. I'm going to have to really get to work, so this" — he held up the stick — "feels natural. I'm used to a different approach."

She smiled. "You'll do fine."

"I hope so," Cris answered. "If —"

"Hey, *Murphy!*" called an unwelcome voice from behind him. Cris turned to see Max and Doog standing a few feet away.

"What's the matter, Murphy, you can't cut

it with the boys?" asked Max. "You playing with the *girl's* team now?"

"Ignore them," muttered Molly, seeing Cris's angry expression. "Don't get into a —"

"Murphy's gonna play hockey with the *girls,*" yelled Doog. "You have to wear a skirt when you play with the girls, *Crissy?*"

The two kept up their taunts until Cris was ready to charge at Max, but Molly cooled him down. "Don't play their silly game," she urged. "If you get into it with them, they've won. Don't even look at them."

It wasn't easy, but Cris kept his back to the boys. When they saw that Cris wasn't going to rise to the bait, Max and Doog finally took off.

But Cris had a bad feeling in the pit of his stomach that he and Max would have to settle things between them . . . one way or another.

Cris spoke to Greg about the problem he'd had with Max, and Greg had been sympathetic. But he also observed that Cris had done the right thing to avoid getting into anything more unpleasant with his old friend.

"As soon as you lose your temper, you'll be playing Max's game," he said. "As long as you don't, you're the winner. It won't last forever."

Meanwhile, Cris continued to practice with the Hawks. He was feeling pretty good about hockey, and his progress with the Hawks. After the first week's practice, Harp had called Mr. Murphy and said some complimentary things about Cris's attitude and potential. He mentioned that the Hawks would play their first game of the season in less than a month. At first, Harp had doubted that Cris would be ready to play, but after seeing him trying so hard, he thought he might get into the game after all.

When he heard that, Cris felt that he had a real goal to aim for.

He hoped that he'd eventually stop missing the fun he had with Max and Doog and the aggro skaters. Max had been a good guy to hang with . . . before he had become a creep. Cris still automatically put his aggro skates in his gym bag with his hockey gear, in case he wanted to try some of his old moves sometime.

But so far, he hadn't been near the halfpipe. He didn't want to risk an encounter with Max. He hated the angry words and that awful feeling in the pit of his stomach that always followed. So he stayed away.

On the plus side, he was enjoying the time he spent with Steve and Molly. They'd gone to the mall a couple of times and listened to music and had some laughs together. Even though he might have lost some friends, he had gained new ones, and they were a good replacement.

Also, he was becoming a pretty decent hockey player, he thought. Harp was encouraging and so was Steve. The hockey stick that had seemed so clumsy and impossible to handle not long before was now no problem at all. He could skate with the puck as fast as several of the other players, though not as fast as Steve or Molly. His agility gave him a knack for switching directions quickly and maneuvering past opponents. A couple of times he'd had the satisfaction of juking Leo almost out of his skates and leaving him behind.

Leo was still not a buddy. He tended to be sarcastic and cutting in his remarks to Cris, but Cris was able to deal with it, sensing that Leo was the kind of guy who would keep prodding him until he had passed some kind of test, after which he'd lighten up. At least the guy wasn't giving him the kind of problems that Max was.

One day, in a three-on-three session, Cris was teamed up with Barry and Molly, with Molly at center and the boys on the wings. He was skating on Molly's left, and Steve came up to try to keep him outside, away from the goal. Suddenly Cris swung to his left, extending his right leg so that the right skate acted like a brake, bringing him almost to a complete stop. As he slowed, Cris bent his left knee and pivoted sharply left, then accelerated, leaving Steve behind. Molly delivered a pass that he took on his stick and hit a wicked slap shot — a shot he had recently started to work on — and the puck slid into the goalmouth!

Molly let out a whoop, and Steve came over, grinning broadly.

"Killer move, my man! You had me totally fooled."

Harp applauded from the sideline, and so did a few other Hawk onlookers. Even Leo nodded approval, though he didn't say a word. *Maybe*, Cris thought, *I just passed his test.*

At the end of practice, Steve came over and said, "I can't believe how fast you've caught on to this game! It's truly awesome."

"That's the truth," Molly added as she came up alongside Steve. "Does it have anything to do with your aggro background?"

Cris shrugged. "I don't know, maybe. Aggro helped my balance and coordination, so . . . I guess."

Molly brightened. "Hey, I'd like to see you

do some of your moves. Could you show me?"

"Sure," Cris said, "any time."

"How about right now?" Molly asked.

Startled, Cris blinked. "Now? I didn't think you meant . . . well . . ."

Molly checked her wristwatch. "Why not? It's pretty early. We could go over to the other side of the park."

"Sounds good to me. I'll come, too," Steve said.

Cris realized, with a sudden chilling feeling, that they would almost definitely run into Max and some of the aggro regulars, not an idea he liked too much. He wondered if he could think of a good excuse to put it off, and then thought, *Why should I? I have as much right to be there as they do. Maybe Max and I could even talk, get to be friends again, or at least stop being enemies.*

"All right," he said at length. "I just have to change into my aggro skates. They're in my gym bag. Then we'll go."

The aggro skates, with their smaller wheels, felt a little funny to Cris after not having worn them for a while. As he skated toward the halfpipes and rails, he wasn't sure whether he wanted to see Max or not.

Well, whatever was going to happen would happen. And it would be fun to show off his old skills for his new friends.

Max *was* there, and stared in surprise and anger when Cris arrived, accompanied by Steve and Molly.

"What are *you* doing here?" he demanded, skating up to Cris.

Cris decided not to get hostile; he'd at least give Max a chance to be cool about this meeting. He pointed to his Hawk teammates. "Thought I'd show these guys what aggro is all about. They're curious."

"Is that so?" Cris saw, with a sinking feeling, that Max was not about to be cool. In fact, Max was obviously already *hot.* He turned to Doog, who had been watching from a distance and didn't look happy about what was happening. "The hockey players are *curious.* Isn't that nice?"

Max smiled in a nasty way, and then the smile disappeared abruptly. "We don't want you here, Murphy, or your friends, either."

"Yo, Max," Doog said, skating up. "Take it easy."

Steve tapped Cris's arm. "Come on, we'll go."

But Cris stared at Max. "This is a public park, and we have a right to be here, too."

Max stepped up to Cris until he was inches away. "Yeah? Well, *I* say you don't."

"*Hey!*" Molly shouted. "Cut it out." She moved toward Max, eyes blazing. "Who do you think you are?"

Max sneered. "Get your girlfriends out of here before there's real trouble."

Cris was about to grab Max, who wanted it to happen, when Steve pulled Cris away. At the same time, Doog grabbed Max and yanked him back, saying, "Don't, man. Chill out!"

"Come on," Steve urged. "This isn't worth it, let's just go, all right?"

Cris took a deep breath and nodded. "You're right, it's not worth it." He turned to Molly and Steve and shook his head. "Sorry."

He skated away with Steve. Molly glared at Max and then followed the boys.

"Keep away from here!" yelled Max. "And stay away from *me!*"

Cris didn't turn back. He found that he was trembling.

Was it anger? Or was it fear that he and Max would never again be friends?

When Cris left school the next day, he was feeling terrible. He had seen Max several times — in hallways, in the cafeteria, in classes — and each time Cris had turned away. Once, during lunch, Max had seen him and started toward him, but Cris hadn't waited. He had walked away. He thought that Max had called out, but the cafeteria, as always, was noisy and it had been impossible to hear what Max wanted.

Maybe Max had wanted to apologize, but Cris believed that it was equally possible that Max had wanted to take matters up where they had been left at the park. Whichever was true — or in any other case — Cris had no desire to have any contact with his ex-friend at all. Max's behavior had been too much, especially in front of Cris's teammates. Doog had seen Cris in the hall and nodded, but not said anything.

Every time Cris thought about what had gone down at the park he felt angry all over again. He'd had trouble getting to sleep the night before, and, in the morning, his mother had asked whether Cris was feeling under the weather. Cris had not said a word about the situation to his parents or Greg. It was his problem to deal with.

When he left school to go to practice, Cris was startled to see Steve and Molly waiting for him outside. They both went to a school in the neighboring town and he usually met them at the park.

"Hey," he said, slapping his friends' hands. "How come you're here?"

Steve shrugged. "We just decided to go over to the park with you, that's all."

Molly shot Steve an irritated look. "That's *not* all," she said. "We wanted to make sure that there were no . . . problems . . . *you* know."

Cris did know, but still put on a look of puzzlement. "What kind of problems?"

"Oh, cut it out," snapped Molly. "With those guys from the park."

Cris grinned. "You mean you came over here to protect me?"

Steve held up a hand. "No way! We don't think you need protection. We just wanted to make sure everything was cool, that you weren't hassled."

"Right," Molly agreed. "We wanted to be here for you, you know . . . for support."

The three teammates started skating toward the park.

Cris felt happy to know that they cared that much about him. Something must have shown in his expression, because Molly peered at him and asked, "You okay?"

"Sure, fine," said Cris. "I was just thinking . . . I'm not used to people worrying about me like this, except for my folks."

"You're all right with it, though, aren't you?" Molly looked anxious, as if she thought Cris might be insulted in some way.

"Absolutely," Cris assured her. "I think it's great. It's only that I'm not used to it."

"It's no big deal," Steve said. "That's what teammates do. Help each other out, watch each other's back, stuff like that."

Cris nodded thoughtfully. "I understand." Then he sighed. "I wish Max could understand. He doesn't get it at all."

Molly scowled. "Oh, *him.* He doesn't

deserve a friend like you. Forget about him."

"The thing is, Max is really a good guy . . . well, he used to be, anyway."

"Maybe he's jealous," suggested Steve.

"Jealous?" Cris considered the idea, which hadn't occurred to him. "Of what?"

"Of you," Steve replied. "Of us. Of you having new friends."

"That doesn't make sense," Cris protested. "Just because I made new friends, that didn't mean I didn't want to hang on to my old ones. I wanted to stay tight with Max and that bunch. But he was, like, a total jerk."

"For sure," Molly agreed.

"Maybe he *is* a total jerk," Steve said. "Or maybe he thought you had turned your back on him, so he got bent out of shape and hurt about that. It's a possibility, anyway."

Cris was quiet for a minute. He realized

that he had been so involved with how Max had hurt *him* that he hadn't even considered the chance that Max felt the same way.

If Max did . . . maybe, just maybe, their friendship wasn't completely over.

Harp finished off practice that day with some three-on-three drills. In one of them, Cris broke away on offense, but couldn't handle a hard pass from Steve and lost a scoring opportunity.

"What's the matter, aggro-boy?" asked Leo, skating alongside. "Miss your half-tubes?"

"They're called half*pipes,*" Cris answered. He was getting used to Leo's routine and didn't let himself get rattled.

"Cris!" Harp called. "You weren't ready for that pass! Don't lose concentration!"

"Sorry, Coach," said Cris, who had been thinking about Max and what Steve had said earlier, and not where the puck was. He resolved to keep his mind on the game.

Could it be that he had hurt Max's feelings without meaning to? Sometimes it was easier to see when your own feelings got bruised than when you did it to someone else.

A few minutes later, Cris fired a pass to Molly at the point, who slapped the puck over to Steve. Cris watched Steve fake a shot and give the puck back to Molly with a backhand pass.

Slick move, Cris thought. *I have to work on my backhanded —*

WHAM!

Cris felt like he'd run into a wall. He struggled to regain his balance, then turned to where the hit had come from. There was Leo, grinning. Leo's body check was an obvious foul, but he wasn't apologetic. Far from it.

"Oops," Leo said. "Clumsy me."

He stood there, as if daring Cris to do something about it, but Cris turned away. He felt foolish, but decided that if he started a fight it would look bad to the coach and the team.

Harp, talking to another player, had missed the whole thing. Otherwise, he'd probably have stopped play and given Leo a lecture, as he'd done once or twice. As Cris skated past Barry, the other Hawk whispered, "Smart move. Find a way to get back at him."

Cris bided his time, and then, shortly before practice ended, had his chance. Once again, he was on an attacking team, and out of the corner of his eye he saw Leo barreling toward him, intent on ramming him again.

Cris pretended not to see Leo until just before they were about to collide. Suddenly he bent his knees and skidded to a stop on the sides of his skates. Leo rocketed past him, smashed into the rail that surrounded the rink, and flipped over to the ground.

As Leo slowly picked himself up, wincing, Cris whispered, "Oops. All that aggro skating's made me clumsy, too."

He turned and skated away, leaving Leo staring after him, unable to do anything about it. As Cris passed Barry, the other boy smiled and winked. For Cris it was a sweet moment. Leo gave him no further trouble that day.

After dinner, Cris was finishing his homework when Greg looked into his brother's room. "How's it going? Making progress?"

"Yeah, I think so." Cris told Greg about what had happened with Leo. Greg smiled. "When I started playing hockey, there were a couple of guys who tested me like that. They wanted to see if I could take it, and also if I would keep my cool. You did the right thing by not getting into a fight, and also in giving him back a little of his own medicine. Bet he lets up on you now."

"You think so?" Cris leaned back in his chair and sighed. "Now if only *Max* would let up on me, everything would be great."

Greg shook his head. "I didn't think Max would keep this up for so long."

Cris told Greg what Steve had suggested, about Max being jealous.

"He may have something, there," Greg said, thinking. "After all, you two were hanging out together all the time for years, and all of a sudden, you find another sport and other friends. He may think you abandoned him."

"But I didn't —"

Greg held up a hand. "I know, that wasn't your idea. But he may think so, anyway. Is there any chance you could get him interested in hockey?"

"*Max?* No way! He hates hockey, for some reason."

Greg shrugged. "Well, it was just an idea. Think about it."

Cris did think about it. But after a while, he gave up. The idea that Max could get involved in hockey seemed impossible.

Harp was busy with other commitments the next day, and the Hawks didn't practice. Cris decided to skate over to where he and Max and their buddies had skated to see if the coast was clear, in which case he'd see if he was rusty or if he could still do some aggro moves.

He was relieved to see that Max was nowhere to be found. In fact there was only one skater in sight, a guy he couldn't recognize. The guy was on the halfpipe, just warming up, skating up the incline, doing a 180 turn, and swooping down the other side.

Nothing spectacular, but whoever it was appeared to be pretty athletic. As Cris came over, the other skater did a really sharp move on the rim of the halfpipe: a backflip, landing on one hand, and then all the way over onto the skates again! Who *was* this stranger? Cris was puzzled, until the guy took off the helmet.

It was Molly!

"Hey!" she said, smiling. She was wearing aggro skates — small wheels, grind plates, and all.

"Hey, yourself!" replied Cris. "I didn't know you did aggro."

"Well, I used to . . . a little, anyway." Molly seemed embarrassed at having been caught.

"'A little!'" echoed Cris. "It looks to me like you can do a *lot!*"

"Well, I was pretty good, I guess," Molly admitted. "But then I discovered hockey, and I preferred it, being part of a team."

"I can understand that," Cris said.

"I was hoping to see you do some moves the other day," Molly said. "How about showing me now? I mean, you've got your aggro skates . . ."

"Sure," Cris said. "That's why I came over here. I just hope I'm not totally out of practice. It's been a few weeks, so don't expect too much, okay? Let's see . . . I'll warm up with a Miszou Grind on the rail there."

Cris skated toward the three-foot-high handrail, leaped, and slid down the rail, his lead skate parallel to the rail and the grind plate of his left, trailing, foot, "grinding" the rail, and dismounted. "Your turn," he said to Molly.

"How about a Makio Grind," she said, heading for the rail. As her right skate hit the rail, she extended her left leg, grabbed and held her left skate, and went the length of the rail on her right foot alone.

"Excellent!" Cris said. "Show me what you can do in the halfpipe?"

Molly did a series of flips and 360s, which Cris applauded. "Now you," she said to him.

Cris grinned. "Okay. If I'm feeling really confident, I'll finish off with a Misty Flip. If I'm not . . . I won't."

"That's pretty heavy stuff," Molly said. Skating over to the top rim of the halfpipe wall, he dropped in, swooping down the side and up the opposite side, did a 180 and came back down. When he reached the top this time, he did a full 360, and came back down fakie, facing backward. On his next pass, he got some extra elevation and spun around one and a half times, for a 540.

Finally, he went up the side wall and did a complete flip and a 540 turn, coming down fakie, beyond the halfpipe: the Misty Flip.

"Amazing!" Molly came over to Cris. "Think I could do that?"

"Probably," said Cris. "You really need to grab a lot of air, and you have to be able to handle the upside down part, but I'll bet you could. Can you do a Farfegnugen?"

"What's that?" asked Molly.

Cris demonstrated a Farfegnugen on the rail. Bending his knees and flexing his ankles, Cris traveled the length of the rail on the leading edges of both grind plates. He knew it looked impressive.

"Neat!" Molly's eyes were shining. "I have to learn that one!"

Cris and Molly went over to a low rail designed for beginners and practicing new moves, and Cris demonstrated it again.

"It feels weird at first. You really have to bend your knees, and your ankles have to be flexed so the edges of your grind plates are on the rail. See?"

Cris did another one. Molly, an excellent natural athlete, picked it up quickly. At her request, Cris ran through a few more moves, including a stylish Kind Grind, and then, on the halfpipe, a dazzling 720 — *two* complete turns off the top of the halfpipe wall.

He was startled to hear some clapping and whistling. Turning, Cris saw that a few other Hawks had arrived in time to watch the last few stunts, including Leo, who looked impressed, although he wouldn't say as much.

"You're pretty good at that stuff," was the most he'd admit.

"Want to learn any aggro tricks, Leo?" Cris offered. "You can impress your friends."

"No, thanks," Leo said. "We'll be starting the season soon and I don't want to get hurt. You guys would be in deep trouble if anything happened to me."

"Uh-huh, right, Leo," Steve said, keeping a straight face. "I've been losing sleep lately, thinking, 'Oh, wow, what if Leo gets hurt?' Thanks for thinking of us."

Cris was happy to see that Leo laughed along with the others. At least he didn't take himself too seriously. Cris also was pleased to feel that he was more and more accepted as part of the team.

"Uh-oh," Molly said, looking over Cris's shoulder. "Here comes trouble."

Cris turned. Max, Doog, and a couple of other aggro skaters were headed their way.

Max stopped short when he saw who was there. His face assumed an expression of total astonishment. "You don't listen real well," he said, hands clenched into fists. "Or your memory is pretty bad. I told you you weren't welcome around here."

"And *I* told *you* that this is a public park and I have as much right to be here as you do," Cris snapped. He was fed up with Max's bullying, and he also knew he had more support this time. "So back off."

"You hockey wusses should have brought those sticks with you," Max said, "because you're gonna need them."

"Hey, everybody, let's cool it," Steve said, stepping in front of the angry Cris. "We don't want —"

"Speak for yourself, dude," snarled Doog, stepping forward and standing next to Max. "If you don't want a piece of us, you better take off, right now." Doog was usually easygoing but he had been pumped up by Max's anger.

"Is that so?" said Leo, getting nose to nose with Max. "Can you creeps do anything but talk big? You want to mix it up a little?"

"Leo! Cut it out!" yelled Cris, alarmed at how things were going. But when Cris put a hand on Leo's arm, Leo shook it off.

"I don't *believe* this!" shouted Molly.

"What's the matter with you?" She pointed a finger at Max. "Are you crazy or something?"

Doog yelled, "If you weren't a girl . . ."

"You'd what?" Molly snapped back. "Don't let that stop you! I'm tougher than you . . . *and* I can skate circles around you, too!"

Doog laughed. "For sure! If you didn't have a hockey stick to hold you up, you'd need *training wheels!*"

"Okay, big shot," said Molly, "let's see who's better! I know you're too dumb and lame for hockey, but this *girl* can beat you at aggro!"

"No way!" Doog said.

"Way!" Molly replied. "You scared to take me on? One against one?"

Max sneered. "Come on, Doog! Show these wimps what a real skater is."

Doog stared at Max. "You want me to compete with a *girl?*"

"Why not?" Max jerked a thumb at her. "It's her idea, right? Go ahead, show her up."

Steve tapped Molly on the shoulder and said, "You don't have to do this."

Molly grinned at him. "I *want* to! I'm going to. Don't worry, it's cool."

"She's really good," Cris whispered to Steve. "And it's better than fighting, right?"

It was agreed that Molly and Doog would go head to head. Molly would do a stunt that Doog would have to match, and then Doog would go first, until there was a clear winner.

Molly started off on a handrail running alongside a set of steps. "I'll start easy — here's a Frontside." She leaped on the rail and slid down with both skates across the rail.

Doog had no trouble doing the same. "How about a Fishbrain?" he said, going back to the top of the steps. He came down the rail on the side of his left skate, holding his right skate with his right hand.

Molly smiled and did the same. "Unity Grind," she said. She slid down the rail, both skates across it — with her legs crossed.

"Pretty good," muttered Doog, who did the Unity, too. He grinned. "Let's see if you can do a Farfegnugen."

Molly and Cris exchanged a smile. Her Farfegnugen was as good as Doog's. Doog was looking nervous. He knew that he was up against a really good skater.

They moved to the halfpipe and did some spins. Doog did a Hand Plant — somersaulting over a rail, planting a hand on it, and finishing the somersault on the other side. Molly followed suit. Molly jumped on the rail in a Frontside, and, in the middle of the rail, turned around so her other skate was in front — a Backside Grind. Doog duplicated it, with a little difficulty. Molly had no trouble matching Doog's 540.

"Can you do a Bio Spin?" she asked. She skated up a ramp near the halfpipe. At the top of the ramp, she went into a backflip and spun around one and a half times, came down fakie, and circled back to Doog.

Doog stood and chewed on his lower lip, not happy at all. But he had no choice. He took a deep breath and began moving, heading up the ramp. At the top, he tried to do a backflip, but lost his balance and came down hard on his back and shoulder.

He lay on the ground, motionless, while everyone looked down at him, horrified.

8

To Cris, it seemed like a long time passed while the group stared at Doog, lying on the pavement.

"Doog?" called Max. He looked around, wildly. "Is he . . . is he *dead?*"

Steve turned to Molly. "Find a pay phone, call nine-one-one, explain what happened, and wait for the ambulance to come. Then show the EMT people where we are."

Molly sped off. Steve knelt next to Doog and looked closely. Then he looked up. "He's alive." He noted that Doog was bleeding from a gash on one arm, and asked,

"Anyone have a clean handkerchief or some kind of cloth?"

Cris dug into his gym bag and pulled out a pair of socks. He quickly handed them to Steve, who placed them on the gash. "Leo, hold this here and keep some pressure on it. That'll control the bleeding."

As Leo followed Steve's instructions, Steve looked at Max. "Give me your jacket."

Max blinked and stood there, paralyzed. "Come on, give me that jacket!" Steve repeated. "He has to be kept warm, to prevent shock."

Max handed the jacket to Steve, who laid it over Doog's legs. "Good thing he was wearing pads and a helmet," he said.

"How is he?" asked Cris.

"I don't know," Steve said. "The medics will give us an idea — he's awake!"

Doog's eyelids fluttered, and he opened his mouth and tried to speak, but nothing came out. He started to raise his head. Steve placed a hand on Doog's uninjured arm.

"Don't move," he said. "Just take it easy." He looked up. "What's his name?"

"His name's Doog," Max said.

Steve nodded. "Doog? Listen, you had an accident. There's an ambulance coming real soon. Meanwhile, take it easy and don't move. You understand? Blink your eyes if you do."

Doog blinked, then closed his eyes. In the distance, Cris heard the ambulance siren. "Here they come," he said.

Doog didn't open his eyes, but he smiled. He said something, so softly that nobody could make it out. Max got down next to him. "What did you say?"

Doog whispered again, and Max looked up. "He says, 'That girl can really skate.'"

A moment later, Molly returned, leading two paramedics and a gurney. The EMT team worked quickly, placing a board under Doog's body, in case he had suffered spinal damage, checking the gash on his arm, and carefully placing him on the gurney.

"It's impossible to say for certain yet," said one of the ambulance team, "but it doesn't seem like his injuries are serious. Which of you guys took care of him till we got here?"

"He did," Max said, pointing to Steve.

"What's your name?" asked the medic.

Steve identified himself.

"Well, Steve," the medic said, "you did great. That bandage was just right, and keeping him warm was the proper thing to do. I'm glad he had pads; if he hadn't had protective gear, it very likely would have been a whole lot worse. I'm speaking from experience.

"Okay, we'll take him to the hospital for X-rays and a thorough checkup."

"Can I come with him?" Max asked.

"Sure," the woman said. "Let's go."

Max followed the gurney to the ambulance. After he clambered in, he reached his hand out to Steve. "Thanks," he said. Steve shook hands and nodded. The ambulance door slammed closed and the vehicle sped away. A couple of Doog's aggro-skating friends, looking shaken, slowly wandered away.

"I better go," Leo said. He was unusually quiet. He started to go but turned back. "Sorry I lost it there, before. I shouldn't do that, I guess." He took off.

"You really know that emergency medical stuff, huh?" Cris said to Steve.

Steve shrugged. "I learned from Harp. He took a course when he started coaching. You know, sometimes there are collisions, guys take falls. Anyway, he taught me some things."

"Lucky you were here," said Molly.

Cris turned to Molly. "We're lucky *you* were here. If you hadn't challenged Doog, there would have been a fight. We might have needed more than one ambulance."

Molly looked at Cris with a more serious than usual expression. "I *hate* fighting. But I'm sorry this happened."

"Not your fault. In fact, if it's anybody's fault, it's mine. I should have ignored Max instead of getting in his face." Cris sighed. "I'll call the hospital later and see how Doog made out."

"Call and tell me, okay?" asked Molly.

"Me, too," Steve said.

"No problem," Cris assured them and turned for home. His ongoing problems with Max suddenly seemed less important.

He couldn't help feeling responsible in a way for Doog's accident. What if Doog was badly injured? Even paralyzed?

That night, he found it hard to eat. He

managed to get food down because he didn't want his parents to worry about him. But he said nothing about Doog, figuring he'd tell them only if Doog was seriously hurt. For sure, his mom would want him to give up aggro skating — maybe forbid him to skate altogether.

Of course, even *that* seemed minor, compared to what might be happening to Doog.

At last, he went to his room to call the hospital. But the hospital wouldn't give him any information since he wasn't a relative.

Cris sat looking at the phone for a moment. He didn't want to disturb Doog or his parents, but he needed to know Doog was okay. There was only one answer. He dialed Max's number.

"Hi," Max said when he got on the line.

"How's Doog?" Cris asked.

"He has a dislocated shoulder and cuts and bruises," Max said. "But he'll be fine."

Cris felt a wave of relief. "I'm glad to hear it. I was worried that — well, you know."

"Yeah, I know," Max said. There was a long pause. Neither one seemed to know what to say. Finally, Max went on. "Tell everyone Doog'll be okay. And tell that guy Steve thanks again."

"Sure," Cris said.

"Well . . . see you, I guess," said Max.

Cris wondered if he should say something more, but couldn't think what it would be. "Yeah. See you."

He hung up.

Cris was still feeling upset the next morning, even though he knew that Doog would be back to normal in a few days. The thought of what *might* have happened was hard to stomach, but he couldn't get his mind off it. He sat by himself to eat lunch, on the lawn behind the school, trying not to think about Doog or the accident. A shadow fell across him and he looked up.

It was Max. Max stood silently for a minute, then finally said, "Hi."

"Hi," Cris replied. There was another long silence.

"I just wanted to make sure that guy Steve knows that I appreciate him helping Doog the way he did," Max muttered.

"I told him last night," Cris said, "and I told him and Molly that Doog was going to be fine. I was really happy to hear that."

"There's something else I want to tell you," Max said.

"What is it?" Cris said, when it seemed that Max would never say another word.

"Just that I'm sorry I was mean to you. I acted like a real jerk. I can understand why you went and got new friends, and I guess that's what I deserve."

Max hurried away before Cris could think of what he wanted to say in return. When Cris got up to go after Max, he was unable to find him. Finally he gave up.

That afternoon, after taking the team through the usual drills, Harp divided the

Hawks into two squads, five against five, the same size as regulation roller hockey teams. Cris was put at left wing on one squad with Molly at right wing. They had worked well together in past practices.

In the first minute of play, Cris had the puck and held it long enough to draw a defenseman toward him, allowing Molly to dart through the opening that was created. Cris faked a shot and flipped a backhand pass to Molly, who took a shot that caromed off the left upright of the goal. Good shot, near miss.

But a minute later, Cris thought he had a chance to get past the defense. He raced forward hoping Barry, at center, would see him and deliver a pass. However, Leo, playing defense, came in and forced Cris away just as Barry tried to get the puck to him. Leo picked off the pass and fired the puck all the way down the rink, where Steve took it and had an easy shot. Cris was out of position and unable to get back and help defend.

"Cris!" Harp called out. "What went wrong there?"

"I couldn't get to that pass," Cris replied, "because Leo rode me off the play."

"You were out of position!" Harp said, cupping his hands so that Cris would hear. "You were trying to go for it all in one move, instead of being patient and setting up a good shot. Remember — you have to play offense *and* defense!"

Cris nodded. There was a lot for him to learn and remember.

A little later on, on defense, Cris saw that Leo was about to pass to Steve. Leo had a way of telegraphing his passes sometimes. Anticipating the pass, Cris cut in front of Steve and picked it off neatly. It looked like a perfect breakaway opportunity and he barreled down the rink, ignoring Barry and Molly. He pulled back his stick, fired a slap shot, and was astonished to see a defender knock the puck away from the goal. He hadn't even seen her coming.

"*Hey!*" called Molly, looking annoyed. "Remember me? Remember Barry? Your *teammates?*"

Cris felt embarrassed, knowing Molly was right to be mad. "Sorry, I thought —"

"You didn't 'think,'" Barry said. "You tried to be a one-man team, and we blew a scoring chance."

"Sorry," Cris said again.

"You seem to say that a lot," Molly said, looking grumpy. "Instead of being sorry, keep your head in the game!"

Cris couldn't argue. She was right.

"We're a team, remember," Molly went on, still mad. "Remember, there's —"

"No 'I' in 'team,'" Cris finished for her. It

was a line Harp used from time to time, and Cris wondered if he should paint it on his bedroom wall, so he'd remember.

Harp's whistle brought play to a halt. "Pretty good, people. Take a ten-minute breather. Cris, you're getting much better, but you are developing some bad habits that we want to nip in the bud. Right?"

"Right," Cris admitted. "I'll work on it, Coach."

Molly skated over to Cris, her anger forgotten. "Hey, look who's here," she said, gesturing toward the benches alongside the rink.

Cris was startled to see Max sitting on a bench. "He's been watching for a few minutes," said Molly. "What does *he* want, anyway?" Her tone of voice showed that she still thought of Max as the jerk who had been hassling Cris.

"He's okay, really," Cris insisted and waved to the boy on the bench.

But when he skated toward him, Max got up abruptly and took off. Cris thought about trying to catch him, but realized that he had to stick around and finish practice. He thought he might call Max that evening and try to reestablish some kind of connection.

When Harp called the team back on the rink, Cris resolved that he would concentrate on avoiding the mistakes he had been making; he'd try to be aware of where the puck was at all times and be a team player.

He managed to play better, he thought afterward. At one point, the goalie on Cris's squad came out of the crease to get the puck, leaving the goal unguarded. Steve made an interception and fired at the open goalmouth, but Cris stretched out a leg at the last second and made a beautiful pad save.

"All *right!*" Leo shouted. It was the first

time Leo had ever said anything complimentary about Cris's play.

On the sideline, Harp clapped. "Way to hustle, Cris!" Cris felt great, forgetting his worries about Max for the time being.

His concentration paid off one other time, too. He was defending against Steve, who was looking for a pass. Steve tried to get clear, but Cris managed to stay between him and the puck for a full minute. Steve was considered a particularly agile skater who could usually break free of defenders. But Cris matched him turn for turn and wouldn't be suckered by Steve's fakes.

When Harp stopped play, Steve was out of breath, an unusual condition for him. He turned to Cris and said, "Man, how did you do that? I threw every move I had at you, and you stuck right in there!"

Cris grinned, feeling like he'd just won a medal. "I was lucky."

Steve reached out a hand for Cris to slap. "Luck had nothing to do with it, dude. That was nothing but tough D."

A few other Hawks congratulated him on his work, and Cris was so pumped, he practically floated home.

He was still feeling great after dinner as he finished his homework, when his mother knocked on his door.

"Honey? Max is here, and he wants to talk to you, if it's all right."

Cris stared in surprise.

Mrs. Murphy said, “Cris, is there a problem between you and Max? Why wouldn’t it be all right for you two to talk?”

“Uh, no, Mom, there’s no problem. No big deal, anyway. Tell him to come on up.”

Max came into the room slowly, as if he wasn’t sure what kind of greeting he’d get. “Hey, how you doing?” He didn’t sit down.

“Okay,” Cris said. “You?”

“All right.”

Neither one looked at the other. Max

looked at the floor, and Cris looked out the window. A long minute went by.

"This is stupid!" Cris said finally, when he couldn't stand the silence anymore. "Sit down, all right? You make me nervous, standing there."

Max sat on Cris's other chair, still looking at the floor. At last, he looked Cris in the eye. "I just want to say, I'm sorry. I've been acting like a real creep. I guess you don't want to be friends anymore, but I wanted to tell you that, anyway."

"I don't know where you got the idea that I don't want to be friends. . . . Well, I guess I *do* know where you got the idea, but . . . it's not true. I still want to be friends."

Max looked a little less gloomy. "Really? Because, I mean, I would understand if you didn't. After what I did."

"Really," Cris answered. "And I think we

both did things, *said* things, that were dumb. It wasn't just you."

Max poked himself in the chest with his thumb. "But *I* started it."

Cris nodded. "Yeah, you did."

Max leaned forward in the chair. "The thing is, when you started with those hockey players, I figured *you* didn't want to be friends, so I . . ."

He trailed off, looking sad.

"Me trying hockey had nothing to do with you," said Cris. "Dad was a hockey player, and Greg plays, and they love it. They'd been getting on me about giving it a shot. I *told* you that."

"I know," Max agreed.

"I figured I could play hockey and still hang out with you and Doog and do the aggro stuff, too. That was my plan. I'd still like to."

"You would?"

Cris smiled. "If I don't, who's going to show you how to do a Fakie 720?"

Max laughed. "Not *you*, dude! You couldn't do a 720 in your dreams!"

"Wrong!" Cris laughed. "In my dreams I can do a 900! Even when you're wide awake, you lose count at 180!"

"Talk is cheap, Murphy! Let's see you do a 720 . . . tomorrow!"

Cris was happy to be able to joke around with Max again. It had been too long.

"There's something else I want to ask you about," Max said. "Do you think I could play hockey?"

Cris's jaw dropped. He looked for a sign that it was a joke, but Max was serious.

Max said, "Close your mouth before a bug flies in."

"Sorry," Cris replied. "You have to admit, that's a weird question, coming from you. You say that hockey is for losers —"

"I know," Max admitted. "That was just me being a jerk. I never even *saw* the game, until yesterday. I put it down because you were interested and I was afraid you'd quit aggro.

"I watched you practice yesterday. Mostly I stayed where you wouldn't see me, because of what had gone down. But . . . well, I *liked* it. Those guys are good skaters."

"How come you watched?" asked Cris.

Max shrugged. "When Doog fell, and that guy Steve took over and made sure that Doog would be all right, I thought, 'This dude is okay.' And I liked how those guys backed you up and were ready to fight for you. It made me think maybe there's more to this 'team' stuff than I thought."

Cris nodded. "You're right. There is."

"Yeah, I see that, now," Max said. "So, I was wondering if there was, like, any chance that I could join your team."

"Join us?" Cris hadn't expected this at all. "I don't know."

Max's face fell. "I guess, after all the stuff I said, there's no way, huh?"

"That's not it, or not all of it," replied Cris. "The thing is, our season starts in a week, and I don't know if you could be ready to play, even if they were willing to let you join. You'd have an awful lot to learn. *I* had an awful lot to learn, and I'm still not all the way there."

"Even if I couldn't play in the games," Max said, "it'd be neat to hang out and learn about it. If it was all right with them, I mean."

"Well, tell you what, I'll ask the coach. And I'll talk with Steve. He's team captain, and if Harp says it's okay and Steve doesn't mind, then I think the others will go along."

Then he frowned.

"Most of the others will go along, anyway.

That dude Leo will probably give you grief. He did with me. But maybe it'll be okay. As far as I'm concerned, it'd be great!"

"You think I could do it?" Max asked.

"Absolutely! You're a great skater. You could pick it up fast. I'll talk to them tomorrow and let you know."

It was during a break in practice the next day that Cris mentioned Max's interest to Harp. Harp knitted his brows. "If he thinks he can really *play,* with the first game only a few days away —"

Cris jumped in. "Max knows he'd have a lot to learn. He hoped he could start learning, work with us, you know . . ."

It sounded lame even as he said it.

Molly, who had been listening, asked, "Isn't Max the dude who was hassling you? *He* wants to play hockey? And *you're* willing to let him? Unbelievable! That guy is a total loser!"

"No, he really isn't," Cris protested. "He came over last night and apologized, and we're friends again. He's not like you think he is, it's . . . it was a mistake, that's all."

"I don't know about any of this," Harp said, "but we have only a few practices before our first game, and we have a lot to do. We don't have time to teach someone new."

The look of disappointment on Cris's face must have been clear to Harp, who added, "If your friend wants to watch practice, he's welcome, and if anyone wants to spend time with him after practice, fine." He walked away.

"Spend time with who?" asked Leo, who, with Steve, had heard only the last part.

"That guy who you almost got into it with the other day," Molly said. "Max. He wants to play hockey all of a sudden. And *he*" — she pointed to Cris — "thinks it's cool!"

"No way!" Leo yelled. "He better stay at his end of the park!"

"Yo, Leo, chill, all right?" Steve said. He looked at Cris. "How come this guy is your good buddy all of a sudden?"

"Max was *always* my buddy," said Cris, "until I started with you guys. Then he got bent out of shape, but he's sorry now. He really is all right, I'm telling you."

"He could have fooled me," Molly said.

"Well, he *is.*" Cris looked around at his teammates. "Here's the thing, okay? If I tell him he can watch us, will you let him? I promise, he'll be fine."

The other Hawks exchanged looks. Finally, Molly said, "If you say he's cool, then I'm willing to let him watch."

Steve nodded. "I don't have a problem."

"He better not give us any trouble," Leo said, scowling. "That's all I can say."

"He won't," said Cris, grinning.

"Let's get to work," called Harp.

A little later, Cris was headed down the

rink, looking for a chance to get a pass from Molly. Leo, on defense, was backing up. Seeing Molly about to pass, he tried to shift over to cover Cris and intercept a potential pass. But his feet got tangled up as he tried to cross over, and he stumbled and sprawled on the ground. Cris, skating fast, couldn't avoid Leo's outstretched leg. He tripped and fell forward. Neither boy was hurt, and both scrambled to their feet as Molly, swerving to avoid the pileup, dropped the puck off for Barry, who fired a shot on goal.

Harp whistled to stop play. "Everyone okay?" he asked. Cris and Leo both nodded. "Good. Molly, good recovery and nice setup for Barry. Everyone, listen up.

"There's an important lesson there. Sometimes, people go down like Leo and Cris just did, on your team or on the opposing team. Unless an official stops play with the whistle, *keep going!* Unless time is called, the puck is still in play, and goals can be scored. If you see that someone might be seriously hurt, ask for time to be called. But if a referee doesn't stop play, you can't stop, either. Clear? Good!"

A thought occurred to Cris, who raised his hand. "Coach? Could I have jumped *over* Leo just then?"

"Hurdled him, you mean?" Harp scratched his head. "I wouldn't encourage that, Cris. It might be dangerous. What if you didn't clear him? It could be nasty."

"The thing is, in aggro — you know, the skating I was doing before I started hockey — we jump pretty high, to get onto rails and to get enough air for flips and stunts like that. I'm certain I would've gotten over Leo, if I'd thought of it."

Harp thought for a moment. "I don't know. . . . Tell you what, let me take a look at what you mean a little later, once we've finished what we have to get done today, all right?

"I want to work on flip shots for a while. If you're looking for a shot and the opposing goalie is sprawled out so he covers most of the bottom of the goalmouth, you can use the flip shot to get the puck over the goalie's body."

Harp demonstrated, putting the blade of the stick in front of the puck, then pulling the handle toward him with his upper hand while using his lower wrist to "flip" the puck up.

He placed a six-inch-high board across the goal and had players try flipping the puck over it. On his first shot, Cris not only cleared the board, but the whole cage!

"Oops!" he said.

"Home runs are good in baseball," Leo drawled, "but they're not much good in hockey."

By his third attempt, Cris had it under control. The backhanded flip shot was trickier, and he resolved to work on it later.

On the whole, though, Cris felt he'd had a good practice. Harp had worked on face-offs early on, placing two players opposite each other and dropping the puck between them, like at the beginning of a game and to restart after play stops. It required lightning reflexes and great stick handling to control the puck and get it to a teammate before your opponent did. Cris found that, among the Hawks, only Steve had a faster stick than he did in face-offs.

He also excelled in defending when attacked by two opponents, instinctively knowing when to target a specific player and when to hang back and force the two attackers to commit.

So he was feeling good when practice ended and was happy to agree when Molly suggested stopping off for some aggro stunts. They found Max there, and Cris told Max what Harp had said.

Max looked disappointed, but insisted that he understood. The three spent a half hour working on grinds, and Molly gave Max a helpful tip on doing a Unity.

When she headed home, the two boys watched her leave. Max turned to Cris. "She may be a girl, but she is *way* cool."

Cris agreed completely.

Max came to practice with Cris the next day and sat on the sidelines. Cris knew that something was wrong from the way the players looked and the subdued tone of their chat.

"What's going on?" he asked Molly.

Molly bit her lip. "Sandy was on her bike and got hit by a car. She broke her leg."

Sandy Thorne was the other girl on the Hawks and Cris hadn't gotten to know her well. She played defense.

"Will she be all right?" asked Cris.

Molly sighed. "She'll have her leg in a cast

for eight weeks and she'll need rehab for another three months. She's out for the season. We're going to see her after practice today."

Cris whistled. "Well, at least she's going to be okay."

Molly nodded. "But that leaves us real thin. Without Sandy, we have only three real defensemen. Barry *could* play there but —"

Cris's eyes widened. He'd had a sudden thought. "Where's the coach?" he asked, looking around.

"On the phone, talking to Sandy's parents," Steve said, joining Molly and Cris. He looked tense and unhappy.

"Listen, how about bringing in Max?" Cris asked. "I know he doesn't know hockey at all, but he's a great athlete and a fantastic skater. Plus, he's built like a defenseman."

Steve looked doubtful. "I don't know. It's crazy to bring in a new guy now."

"Oh, I know Max couldn't play the first

game," Cris said. "But he'd have two weeks to get ready for the *second* game. I picked up a lot of it in two weeks, and I bet he could, too. You think the coach would go for it?"

Molly and Steve looked at Max. "Well," said Molly, "he *does* look like a defenseman. He's solid, kind of like Leo. And he can skate."

"Okay," Steve interrupted, "but the dude doesn't know which end of a hockey stick you hold. He's totally ignorant about the game. Cris, at least you'd watched your brother play hockey. Max has never seen a game."

Molly poked Steve with an elbow. "Here comes Coach. Let's ask him."

Cris, Molly, and Steve ran up to Harp as the man stuck a cell phone in his pocket. "I heard about Sandy," Cris said. "That's terrible."

Harp ran a hand through his hair. He looked tired. "Well, she'll be back to normal eventually, so it could have been worse. I think Barry will have to play some defense."

Molly said, "We were thinking . . ."

"Maybe this sounds crazy . . . ," Cris said.

Steve took over. "Coach, maybe Cris's friend can fill in for Sandy. Not right away, that is . . . but in two weeks, for our second game?"

Harp shook his head. "I don't see how. There'd simply be too much for him to learn."

"He's a great skater," Cris said.

"We'd work with him, put in extra time," Molly added.

"We could give him some of our old gear and pads," offered Steve. "He looks like a defenseman to me."

The coach looked at the three players.

"You'd have to really help out — a lot.

And he'd have to be ready for some hard work."

"He's ready," Cris assured him. "And he's a quick learner."

Harp used his whistle to call the team together. "You all know about Sandy and the problem we're left with. A few of you have come to me with a suggestion.

"Yesterday, Cris told me about this friend of his who was hoping to play hockey. Like Cris, he's a good aggro skater."

Leo groaned. "You're kidding me."

"Got another idea, Leo?" Harp asked. "We're down to three defensemen as things stand. That means that you'd have to play an awful lot. Even if we switch Barry over, we're thin. We'll meet teams with up to twelve players. They'll be fresh when we're out of gas. Another body would mean a big difference."

"Yeah, but . . . ," Leo started. He stopped, realizing that he had nothing to say.

"I won't do anything unless the team approves of it," Harp said. "My own gut feeling is, if this guy can help us, and if he's willing to give it his best shot, we should go for it. But you understand if we do, it'll mean that you'll have to pitch in and give . . . what's his name?"

"Max," Cris said.

Harp nodded. "Give Max your support and help. So, whatever the story may be behind your feelings, Leo, you'll have to put it behind you and start from scratch. What do you say?"

Steve spoke first. "I say, let's do it."

Molly, Barry, and several others agreed. Finally, with everyone staring at him, Leo said, "Okay, yeah. I guess."

"Max!" called Harp. "Would you come here, please?"

Looking puzzled, Max walked over.

"We have a problem, and we're hoping you can help us out," Harp said.

Max looked at Cris, hoping for a clue. But Cris just smiled.

"One of our players is hurt and won't be able to play this season," Harp continued. "I'm told you're interested in giving hockey a try."

Max's eyes grew huge. "Sure! I mean, uh, yes sir, I definitely am!"

Harp fixed his eyes on Max's face. "You certain about this? Because if you say yes, you'll have a lot to do and a lot to learn."

"I'm certain!" Max looked around at the team. "If you guys help me out and give me a chance, I promise I'll give it a hundred and ten percent! That's the best I can say."

Harp nodded. "That's all anyone can ask. All right, then, let's get organized."

Steve gave Max his old stick, and another player had a pair of skates he wasn't using anymore. He bicycled home to get them, while Barry got his spare helmet out of his backpack. Before long, Max had the gear he needed to start learning the game.

While Harp took the rest of the Hawks to begin their regular warmup drills, Steve and Cris stayed with Max. Max had the same difficulty working with the stick in his hands that Cris'd had at first, but he insisted that he would work on it until he felt comfortable.

He wasn't quite as good at skating backward as Cris, nor was he as quick to shift from forward to backward, or cross one leg over the other. But Steve and Cris worked on these skills with him, and Cris saw that Max was an apt pupil who would soon absorb the basics.

Max worked on the swizzle and soon had it down. He skated up and down the rink with the puck. It looked like he'd be quicker at this than Cris had been; Cris'd had a tendency to lose the puck or kick it away accidentally, but Max didn't make those mistakes.

With Cris alongside, Max tried passing the puck back and forth. This proved more challenging; Max had a tendency to either smack the puck way out of Cris's reach or to "fan" on the puck, swinging at it and missing altogether. When he did this, his face turned red and he skated back to get the puck, shaking his head.

"Relax!" called Steve. "You're doing fine, don't get impatient. This is only the beginning."

"Yeah," Max replied, "but there's not much time for me to get it all."

"You're doing better than I did at first," Cris assured his friend, which cheered Max up.

"You're not going to play our first game,"

said Steve, "and there's two weeks till the next one. You have lots of time."

Max looked at Steve, not smiling. "I'll get it. You'll see. I *will.*"

Cris and Steve exchanged a glance. They both hoped Max was right.

Max *did* learn fast. He was able to start working with the rest of the team within a week, as a defenseman. But for the first game of the year, in which the Hawks would play the Rockets, another local team, Max would have to root from the bench. For that game, Barry was made a defenseman, and Harp told Cris that he would play a lot more than he might have expected to if Sandy hadn't been hurt.

In his new gold and maroon Hawk jersey, Cris felt nervous but ready. He hoped he wouldn't embarrass himself on the rink, which was important, especially since his family would be there. Mr. Murphy and Greg knew their hockey, and Cris wanted them to feel proud of him.

At the opening face-off, however, Cris sat next to Max on the bench. Steve and Molly were the forwards, with Leo and Barry on defense. The Rockets, wearing black and orange, took the opening face-off. They moved the puck toward the Hawk goal, using quick, short passes. The Hawk defense shifted back and forth, trying to keep the Rockets to the outside and to keep between the puck and the goal.

Steve poked the puck away from a Rocket forward, and Leo pounced on it and sent it whizzing down the rink, where Molly picked it up. However, her attempted pass to Steve was off-target and the Rockets took over again. To Cris, the Rockets seemed better prepared and the Hawks looked uncertain and not at their best. The Rockets kept the puck in the Hawk zone, playing deliberate offense, looking to catch the Hawks out of position.

Finally, a lightning-fast series of passes sent the puck to a Rocket forward just behind and to the right of the Hawk goal. The Rocket forward slapped the puck to her teammate stationed only a few feet from the Hawk goalie's stick. The goalie moved out to cut down the angle of the shot he assumed was coming. But instead, the Rocket sent a pass across the rink to a defenseman, who now had a shot on a wide-open goal.

Molly saw the threat and darted toward the cage to protect the goal. She managed to block the shot, but it caromed off her skate, directly to another Rocket, who flipped the puck into the net for a goal. The score was Rockets 1, Hawks 0.

Harp made a substitution, sending Cris in

for Molly, who was upset at what she saw as a mistake on her part. On the face-off, Steve got to the puck first and sent it over to Barry, who moved across the center red line and into the attacking zone. Cris flanked him on the right, with Leo behind and to Barry's left.

A Rocket defender moved alongside Cris, trying to ease him toward the side of the rink and out of the play. But as Cris pivoted, he saw Steve race forward into the gap the Rocket defender had left, where Barry's pass found him.

Cris feinted the Rocket player out of position and moved in toward the Rocket goal. Steve fired a short pass to Cris, who passed it to Leo at "the point," near the red line, just inside the Hawks' attacking zone. Leo was now in position to see the whole zone, and sent a hard pass skimming along the rink to Steve. Steve dropped a backhand pass to Barry, stationed behind him. Using Steve as a screen, Barry aimed a shot at the corner of the goal. The puck flew just under the stick of the lunging Rocket goalie. The score was tied, 1–1!

It remained 1–1 for the rest of the first fifteen-minute period. Two more fifteen-minute periods remained.

Cris played a little more than half the first period and was panting for breath at the end. He noticed that the Rocket coach was substituting freely, and that their players were in better shape when time ran out.

Early in the second period, Barry tried a risky crossrink pass to Cris that was picked off by a Rocket, who saw a chance for a breakaway and an easy shot. Cris whirled and took off in pursuit. The Rocket player was unaware of Cris rapidly closing the distance between them, while the Hawk goalie set himself to block the Rocket forward's shot. However, just as the forward pulled back his stick, Cris put on a last burst of speed, hooked the puck with his own stick, and fired it backhand, away from the dangerous area near the Hawk goal.

Molly, skating off the red line, picked up the loose puck. She passed to Barry, who faked a shot and passed to Cris. Cris sent a hard slap shot straight for the goal. But the Rocket goalie sprawled on the ground and smothered the puck under his body, stopping play. The score remained tied.

A few minutes later, Cris made the kind of mistake he had tried to avoid in practice: he got too far ahead of the play, looking for a chance at an easy shot. When the Rockets intercepted a pass, Cris found himself out of position, giving the Rockets a one-player advantage. Before he could recover and get back to help on defense, the Rockets had scored, giving them a 2–1 lead.

Harp took Cris out a minute later, replacing him with Molly. As she headed out, she said, "You were just being offense-minded," but Cris knew better.

Harp came up behind him and bent over to whisper, "What happened to your concentration? Got to keep your mind in the game."

Cris could only agree. Max punched Cris's arm lightly and said, "We'll get it back," but Cris still felt bad about his mistake.

Just before the end of the second period, Cris came back in for Barry, who was wiped out, playing both forward and defense.

Steve, playing at one forward slot, sent the puck rocketing into the Hawk attack zone. Cris raced after it, but a Rocket defenseman came up to block his path. The defender held his stick sideways, and it looked like Cris wouldn't get by him. Suddenly Cris dropped low on one leg, his other leg extended forward. His forward momentum carried him *under* the startled player's stick!

As the player scrambled to get between Cris and the goal, Cris rose and swerved for the puck. The Rocket goalie never had a chance. Cris rammed the puck into the goal to tie the score at two goals apiece. Cris pumped a fist in the air as his teammates raced over to slap him on the back and exchange high fives. His family jumped up and cheered loudly, as the second period ended.

"What was that?" Leo demanded as the Hawks reached the bench. "What did you do out there?"

"*Fishbrain!*" yelled Max, with a huge grin on his face.

Leo spun around to face him. "*What?* What did you call me?"

"Take it easy, Leo, he didn't call you anything," Cris said quickly. "What I did out there — we call that a Fishbrain in aggro skating. Except in a Fishbrain you grab your skate, and I didn't."

Harp shook his head. "Never saw anything like that, but it's legal. Great play, Cris! Heads up, everyone! We have a period left, so keep your heads in the game!"

Harp gathered everyone close. "You can bet that the Rockets will take advantage of their deep bench and bring in plenty of substitutes. Let's pace ourselves and give it everything we have. The idea is not to waste energy with a lot of needless rushing around. Wait for good chances and then play for all we're worth. Keep up the good work!"

Cris went out to start the final period determined that he'd do his part in keeping the Hawks in the game — maybe even winning it, though they were the underdogs. He and Molly stayed inside the Rocket forwards, using their bodies to keep them from getting close to the Hawk goal, and whenever possible, sending the puck back into the Rocket defensive zone. When Cris came out after almost five full minutes, he was tired and winded — but the Rockets hadn't scored.

A minute later, Steve broke away with the puck when the Rockets got careless. They had assumed that the Hawks were going to stay on the defensive from now on. Leo set the breakaway up with a beautiful poke check, taking the puck away from a Rocket forward and putting it directly in front of Steve, who took off before the Rockets could react.

But Steve's shot hit the upright that framed the Rocket goal on the right and bounced away. Barry, who had trailed Steve on the play, pounced on it and slammed it past the Rocket goalie for a score.

The Hawks had taken a 3–2 lead! Cris,

Max, and Molly jumped up and screamed for joy. Could they possibly win this game? What an upset that would be!

But the Hawks were all running out of gas, and two minutes later, with Cris and Molly back in the game, three Rockets set up in their attacking zone, using quick passes to finally draw Barry out of position. All Cris could do was watch in frustration as a Rocket forward swerved past the goal-mouth and put in a perfect backhanded shot to even the score once more, at three goals apiece.

Now it was the Rockets' turn to cheer while Cris and his teammates watched in silence. The score remained tied until the last minute of the third period. The Rockets, once again, were on the attack. Cris was on the rink, backing up and watching one of the opposing forwards bearing down on him.

Suddenly, the other Rocket forward, who

had been behind the one Cris was guarding, veered sharply toward the goal. Screened by his man, Cris didn't see her until she was just to the side of the goalmouth. Neither Leo nor Barry was in position to block her or take her out of the play. A Rocket defenseman got the puck to her with a blazing pass. The Hawk goalie lunged forward, but the Rocket made a flip shot to put the puck over the goalie's arms and stick.

The Rockets led by a goal, with less than a minute to play. Harp pulled the Hawk goalie out of the game, hoping that the team could score with an extra forward on the rink. But instead, a Rocket intercepted a pass and scored again, putting a shot through the unguarded goalmouth. The Rockets won, 5–3.

Cris skated to the sideline feeling awful, unable to look at his family, thinking his error had cost the game. Steve patted his arm.

"It wasn't your fault, man. We were outnumbered. You played great."

But nothing Steve or Molly, or even Leo, said could console Cris until Max came over, frowning.

"Hey, dude, I'm confused, here. I thought this was a *team* game."

Cris looked up. "It *is!*"

"Well, if it's a team game," Max said, "then we win or lose as a team, right?"

Cris had to smile. "Right. You're absolutely right. Thanks."

Max smiled back. "I learned it from you."

13

The following week, the Hawks would face the Mustangs, a team that had been the toughest in the league the previous year. But the Hawks hoped that Max would be ready to play, at least *some* minutes, and take some of the pressure off the others.

Like Cris, Max now had a full set of pads and had gotten his own stick — graphite, just like Cris's — and hockey skates with bigger wheels. He had been almost as quick as Cris to learn how to handle the stick and the puck, and certainly looked like a potential defenseman, with his blocky build and aggressive attitude.

The trick for Max was not to get *too* aggressive. During one practice, he had put a jarring body block on Leo, who hadn't liked it at all. Harp had stopped the practice immediately when the two boys faced each other with clenched fists.

"Settle down, you two!" he said, stepping quickly between them. "Right now!"

"You see what he did?" Leo demanded. "He'd be kicked out of a game for that hit! And he'd have it coming, too!"

"He's right about that," Harp said, looking seriously at Max. "That's what we call 'body-checking,' and it'll get you a penalty plus a game misconduct. That means you'd be out for the rest of the game. And we'd be short-handed again."

Max looked at the ground. "I didn't know

that," he muttered. "I don't know that stuff yet."

"He's not a hockey player!" yelled Leo, still hot. "The guy is just an aggro clown, he doesn't get what being on a team means!"

Steve quietly put a hand on Leo's arm. "Chill, man," he said.

"When I was new, you gave me a shot just like that," Cris pointed out. "Remember?"

Harp was startled, because he hadn't seen it. "That so? Did you, Leo?"

Leo started to speak, thought better of it, and then said, "I guess," in a gruff voice. Then louder, "But it wasn't on purpose! I mean, I didn't . . ."

"Hmm," Harp said, looking at both boys. "Well, I know that you'd never be foolish enough to body-check in a game situation, right Leo?"

"No way!" Leo replied. "Never!"

"As for you, Max," said Harp, "I'll assume you simply haven't had the chance to study the rules yet. So I'm going to give you a manual that has all the rules, the penalties, all the things you have to know, and you're going to take it home tonight and study it. *Hard.* Right?"

"Right," Max agreed.

"And this won't happen again, even in practice," Harp continued. "With either of you, right?"

Leo and Max nodded.

"Excellent," Harp said. "You're both competitors, and I appreciate that. But you're teammates, not opponents. And right now, you're going to shake hands and put this behind you and get back to work."

The boys looked at each other, and Leo stuck out his hand. Max shook it and smiled. "Sorry about that."

Leo smiled back. "You can really hit."

"I bet you can, too," Max answered, "but I hope you never get to show me."

Steve came over to Cris. "Max is going to be okay, isn't he? I mean, he'll be cool in a game, right?"

Cris smiled. "Max is a lot like Leo. He might do something dumb now and then, but he won't do anything stupid in a game." He followed his friend with his eyes. "You know, I think he really does believe in being part of the team."

Cris was surprised to see Leo taking Max aside and working with him on a couple of defensive moves, like the stick lift. Leo had Max act the part of a forward moving with the puck. Coming up to front him, Leo deftly slid his stick under Max's stick and lifted it away from the puck, which he took away! He had Max try it a few times, until Leo was satisfied that Max fully understood the maneuver.

He also worked with Max on shifting from forward to backward skating, an important defensive skill. During breaks, Leo and Max began hanging out together. After practice one day, Cris and Max were going home, and Cris said, "You and Leo are getting pretty tight, huh?"

"Yeah, Leo's pretty cool," Max said. "I may show him some aggro stuff one day. I could loan him my spare skates."

Cris just grinned. Leo learning aggro? That he'd have to see!

The day before the game against the Mustangs, Harp had Max play defense against two attacking forwards, Molly and Steve. The object of the drill, Harp explained, was to make sure that Max didn't commit too soon by coming up on one forward, thus freeing the other one for a shot opportunity. Max did well, keeping his distance, and then using his body to edge Steve toward the side of the rink when Steve tried to make an inside move.

Afterward, Steve came over to Cris and said, "He's looking good." Cris grinned and was happy to see Leo and Max bumping forearms, which was Leo's way of saying "Good work."

At the end of practice, Harp called the Hawks together. "Tomorrow is a big day, so get plenty of rest. The Mustangs are a well-coached team, and Stew Dupont is an excellent goalie, so we have to try to shut them down offensively.

"That's why I'm happy to see that Max is going to be a factor in our game tomorrow. Congratulations, Max, you've come a long way in a short time. All right, see you tomorrow afternoon."

As Max skated home with Cris, he turned to his friend, and asked, "You know how I feel right now? Like the day I did my first

540! I never thought I'd actually be able to play tomorrow!"

"Well, maybe *you* didn't, but *I* always knew you would," Cris said. "When you want to do something, you get it done. You're a Hawk now."

Max's smile faded. "I hope I don't mess up. I'd hate to let you guys down. I mean, I'm still pretty new to this."

"You'll do fine," said Cris. "I just want to not make any dumb mistakes, like last game. If I can keep from doing any of those goofs, I'll figure I did a good job."

Max gave his friend a deadpan stare. "Well, if you *do* mess up, I'll be there to bail you out."

Then he began to laugh.

Cris looked at him and started to laugh, too.

"You are *such* a dweeb," he said.

It was game day. Cris's family was in the stands, along with Max's parents and sister.

There was a big crowd of Mustang rooters, who had come in a convoy of cars and buses. Cris had come to the rink in his uniform with Max, Steve, and Molly.

As he looked at the people, some with banners and signs rooting on their teams, Cris felt his stomach lurch. Would he make any costly errors? Would Max lose his cool? Could they beat these guys and even their record?

"Hey, dude." Seeing the nervous expression on Cris's face, Max had come over to try to make him feel better. "Relax. You're going to do fine, and so am I. It'll all be cool, really. Right, Molly?"

Molly, however, said nothing. She looked grim and stared straight ahead, at nothing in particular.

"Is Molly mad at me?" Max asked.

Steve shook his head, grinning. "Molly's always this way before a game. We call it 'getting her game face on.' She won't talk to anyone, won't look at anyone. As soon as we start to play, she snaps out of it."

Cris couldn't understand how Steve could be so cool and relaxed. The Hawks' team captain looked like he was not going to be doing anything especially important or exciting.

"Hey, Hawks! Over here!" Harp was standing by the Hawk bench and waving toward the players, who were scattered around in small groups. The Mustangs, in their bright yellow and green jerseys, were grouped around their coach. Cris thought they looked pretty lame.

"Listen up, everyone!" Harp looked at a clipboard he held, and continued. "We can beat these guys. The important thing is to keep our heads in the game all the time. Last year they beat us twice, and this year they're two and zero and haven't given up a goal yet. But they can be beaten. True, they have a great goalie, but I don't think their offense is as good as last season. They've lost two top forwards from that team.

"On defense, we need to force them outside as much as we can, and be aware of where everyone is on the rink. On offense, the best way to score on this goalie is to play as a *team,* not to try to be heroes. Set up offensive patterns, keep the puck moving, and look for your openings. Watch out for dangerous passes! Short passes are best — these guys tend to pick off the long ones and turn them into scores."

As Harp said this, Cris thought the coach was looking directly at him; he swallowed nervously.

Harp went on. "When you see an opening, when a Mustang looks to be out of position, that's the time to make our move! I'll bring in substitutes as often as necessary, so don't worry about getting tired. We have the depth this week."

Cris went to the bench with Max as the two starting teams met on the rink and shook hands all around. As the referee held the puck between Steve and a Mustang forward for the face-off, Max turned to Cris. His face looked panicky.

"I can't remember anything! I can't remember what I'm supposed to do!"

Cris said, "Sure you can! I felt the same

way last week, and I guarantee you, it'll all come back as soon as the game starts."

Max stared for a moment, and then nodded and seemed to relax.

On the face-off, Steve controlled the puck. He flipped it back to Leo, who carefully moved it into the attacking zone. The Hawks followed their coach's instructions perfectly, keeping their passes controlled and never trying for a shot on goal when no shot had presented itself. After a couple of minutes, they hadn't taken a shot, and a Mustang defenseman poke-checked the puck away from Molly, sending it to one of his forwards.

Immediately, the Hawks dropped back on defense, spreading themselves out and each picking up an opposing player. When a Mustang suddenly seemed to break free inside and raced toward the goal, Leo came up alongside her and executed a perfect stick lift, taking the puck away and starting the Hawks on offense again. This time, the Hawks actually managed a couple of shots, but the Mustang goalie picked off both, one with his stick and the other with a glove save.

The game remained scoreless, with very few shots taken. Halfway through the period, Harp sent Cris and Max in for Molly and Leo, who needed a rest.

Max sent a hard pass rocketing toward Steve at the red line in the middle of the rink. Steve turned to the attack zone and fired the puck to Cris on the right wing. Cris skated toward the goal. But his progress was blocked by a defender, so he sent a backhanded pass to Barry, who was trailing on the play.

Two Mustangs moved in on Barry. Cris, seeing an opening develop inside, headed for it. But when Barry tried to get the puck to Cris, a Mustang intercepted it, and suddenly Cris realized that he was too far forward to get back quickly. The Mustangs had a one-player advantage!

As Cris hustled to get back, a Mustang took a long shot toward the Hawk goal. Max dived forward, skidding on the rink surface and blocking the puck with his pads, to the cheers of the Hawk rooters. The Hawks moved back on offense, and the scoreless battle continued.

But a minute later, Molly, who had come in for Steve, took a pass from Max and sped across the red line, with Cris alongside. A Mustang defenseman came up beside Cris and attempted to force him away from the inside route, to the side of the rink. Cris bent his knees and flexed his ankles, as if he were doing a Farfegnugen on a rail. But instead of going into a grind, Cris came to a stop. The defender shot past him. Cris cut inside, took a perfect pass from Molly, and moved in on the Mustang goalie.

The goalie came out of the crease to cut down the angle for a shot. Cris "deked" him, swerving as if he wanted to shoot for the side of the goal to Cris's left. The goalie moved with the fake, and Cris swung sharply to his right and poked the puck past the goalie into the net for a score.

The Hawks led, 1–0! The Hawk fans erupted in cheers as the players leaped from the bench yelling.

At the end of the first period, players surrounded Cris, pounding him on the back.

"Okay, what was *that* move?" Leo asked. "Another fish-thingy?"

"Farfegnugen!" Max cheered. "Except instead of grinding, you stopped! Beautiful!"

"I don't know what you're talking about," Leo said, "but whatever it was, it was *awesome.*"

The second period began much like the first one had, with few shots and no scores. Barry and Steve took a couple of shots, but they were blocked, one on an acrobatic lunge by the Mustang goalie.

Halfway through the period, the Mustangs were attacking the Hawk goal. One of their forwards took a snap shot from fifteen feet away from the Hawk goal. It was wide of the net, but took an incredibly unlucky bounce off Barry's skate and tumbled past the Hawk goalie into the net to tie the score.

There was no further scoring in that period. Barry was upset about the goal having come off his skate, but Harp and Steve assured him that he had done nothing wrong.

Just before the third period face-off, Harp clapped his hands for attention. "All right!

You scored against the Mustangs! That's the first goal they've allowed this year, and you can do it again! Just keep up your good work and stay focused!"

Cris was relieved to be able to rest a bit at the beginning of the period. He had played a good deal of the game so far, and needed a break. He cheered when Max made a fine defensive play, faking toward one Mustang forward and then shifting quickly to block a pass to the other one. But the offensive rush started by Max's move didn't result in a goal. Molly's shot was just wide of the net.

A couple of minutes later, the Mustangs were on the attack again. Leo and Max were in together, facing two opponents. One Mustang surprised Max by darting past him toward the goal. The other player had the puck and immediately drove a pass toward the first.

Max, acting by aggro reflex, stuck out his left leg, in a maneuver that looked like what aggro skaters call a Fishbone. The puck hit his knee pad and bounced toward the side of the rink. Another Mustang picked it up, skated around behind the goal, and hooked the puck in past the goalie's save attempt, putting the Mustangs ahead, 2–1.

Max, unhappy and breathing hard, was replaced by Steve. With time becoming critical, the Hawks began to mount a pressing attack, taking several shots that were either wide or blocked, thanks to the lightning reflexes of the Mustang goalie.

It was still 2–1 with one minute left in the game. Harp took out the Hawk goalie and sent Max in to give the Hawks a one-player advantage in the attacking zone.

The Hawks began a quick passing attack, trying to catch the Mustangs out of position and set up a scoring chance. Then a Mustang stuck her stick out, picked off the puck, and started toward the empty Hawk goal!

Max whirled around and started after her. He used a well-timed stick lift to steal the puck back, taking it across the red line into the Hawk attacking zone. Spotting Cris, Max backhanded the puck to him. Cris saw two Mustangs headed for him and realized that someone had to be open. He pivoted, keeping the puck away from the Mustangs on either side of him — and there was Steve, all by himself, just alongside the Mustang goal!

Cris slapped the puck toward Steve, who came out to meet it. He made a feint to his left to draw the goalie to the side and then took a step to his right. As the goalie desperately flung himself across the goal, Steve flipped the puck over him, just under the top bar of the goal! The Hawks had tied the score at two, with only twelve seconds remaining!

The crowd was on its feet, cheering both teams on as they lined up for a face-off. Harp brought his goalie back in, sending Max racing to the bench. The referee dropped the puck. Steve got to it first and backhanded it to Molly.

Molly shot it into the Mustang end of the rink, and before anyone could reach it, time ran out. The Hawks had tied the Mustangs, previously unbeaten and unscored-on, 2–2!

The players from both teams shook hands, and Cris and Max waved happily to their cheering families. Harp raced out and began shaking hands and hugging his players, after shaking hands with the opposing coach.

"Pizza time!" he shouted. "The coach is paying!"

The Hawks cheered and filed off the rink. Cris and Max were in the middle of the happy group, and exchanged a big grin. They were part of a team now, and they had surprised a team that had won every game for over a year. It felt really great.

Leo skated over to Cris and Max and shouted, "Hey, I want to learn some of this aggro stuff! That Fishface and Farvernoogy, and everything!"

"Fish*brain,* and Fish*bone,*" Cris corrected.

"And it's *Farfegnugen,*" said Max, laughing.

"Whatever, I want to learn it. You have to teach me, man!"

"What're you asking *him* for?" Molly yelled, coming between Max and Cris. "I can skate better than both these guys put together! *I'll* show you!"

Leo shrugged and looked around at the other three.

"Tell you what," said Max, "we'll *all* teach you."

"Right!" Cris said. "It's called 'being a team!'"

Matt Christopher

Sports Bio Bookshelf

Kobe Bryant

Terrell Davis

John Elway

Julie Foudy

Jeff Gordon

Wayne Gretzky

Ken Griffey Jr.

Mia Hamm

Tony Hawk

Grant Hill

Derek Jeter

Randy Johnson

Michael Jordan

Tara Lipinski

Mark McGwire

Greg Maddux

Hakeem Olajuwon

Briana Scurry

Sammy Sosa

Tiger Woods

Steve Young

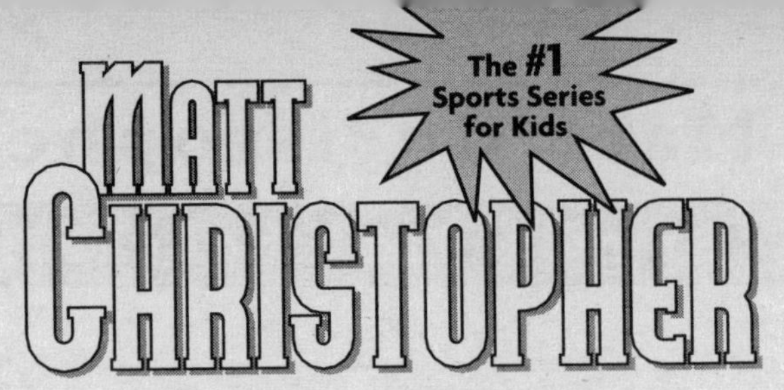

Read them all!

- Baseball Pals
- Baseball Turnaround
- The Basket Counts
- Catch That Pass!
- Catcher with a Glass Arm
- Center Court Sting
- Challenge at Second Base
- The Comeback Challenge
- Cool as Ice
- The Counterfeit Tackle
- Crackerjack Halfback
- The Diamond Champs
- Dirt Bike Racer
- Dirt Bike Runaway
- Double Play at Short
- Face-Off
- Football Fugitive
- The Fox Steals Home
- The Great Quarterback Switch
- The Hockey Machine
- Ice Magic
- Inline Skater
- Johnny Long Legs
- The Kid Who Only Hit Homers
- Long-Arm Quarterback
- Long Shot for Paul
- Look Who's Playing First Base
- Miracle at the Plate
- Mountain Bike Mania
- No Arm in Left Field

Olympic Dream

Penalty Shot

Pressure Play

Prime-Time Pitcher

Red-Hot Hightops

The Reluctant Pitcher

Return of the Home Run Kid

Roller Hockey Radicals

Run, Billy, Run

Shoot for the Hoop

Shortstop from Tokyo

Skateboard Renegade

Skateboard Tough

Snowboard Maverick

Snowboard Showdown

Soccer Duel

Soccer Halfback

Soccer Scoop

Spike It!

The Submarine Pitch

Supercharged Infield

The Team That Couldn't Lose

Tennis Ace

Tight End

Too Hot to Handle

Top Wing

Touchdown for Tommy

Tough to Tackle

Wheel Wizards

Wingman on Ice

The Year Mom Won the Pennant